GRUMBLE DAY

For Dariya and Max – K.G.

For Erica Margaret Veronen Pehrson – S.M.

Text Copyright © 1993 by Kate Green
Illustrations Copyright © 1993 by Steve Mark
Published by The Child's World, Inc.
123 South Broad Street, Mankato, Minnesota 56001
All Rights Reserved. No form of this book may be
reproduced or transmitted in any form or by any means,
electronic or mechanical, including photocopying,
recording, or by an information storage and retrieval system
without express permission in writing from the publisher.
Printed in the United States of America.

Distributed to schools and libraries
in the United States by
ENCYCLOPAEDIA BRITANNICA EDUCATIONAL CORP.
310 South Michigan, Ave.
Chicago, Illinois 60604

Library of Congress Cataloging-in-Publication Data

Green, Kate,
    Grumble day / story by Kate Green
    Summary: A volcano spews out smoke and ash, making all the dinosaurs irritable and
cranky.
    ISBN 0-89565-870-4
    [1. Gratitude – Fiction.   2. Dinosaurs – Fiction.]   I. Title
PZ7.G82354Gr   1992
[Fic] – dc20   91-46506
                                                                        CIP
                                                                        AC

GRUMBLE DAY

Being Grateful

Story by Kate Green
Illustrations by Steve Mark

Every year it was the same.
We couldn't seem to help it.
I woke early
and peered out of my blue cave
at the red volcano.
It was heating up for a rumble
with the sound of a giant grumble.
It happened every year on this day,
spewing smoke and raining sparks
like shot-high stars.
It covered all the shiny plants
with a thick sludge of ash.
And when that smoky ash fell down,
a frown would take over
the whole town.

"T-Bone!" I heard my mother call.
"Breakfast! Get Up!"
"But it's Grumble Day," I moaned.
I didn't want to move.
I knew what was coming.

Out the cave-hole we saw
the first plume of smoke
soar down over us.

My mother threw up her claws.
"Argh," she grumbled,
wrinkling her face.
She crinkled her otherwise-beautiful
dinosaur snout
into a sour, jag-toothed whine.

"Breakfast, again. Each day it's the same,"
she snarled. "Cook, serve, and clean
for two cranky boys
and one slow daughter
who ought to have her hair braided up by now,"
she snorted.

Buddy Rocks and Boulder, my brothers who were usually busy bothering me all through the meal, sulked in silence. They stuck out their lower lips in a murky pout.

Father lumbered
from the back of the cave.
He stretched and glowed
with the small spark of a smile,
until the smoke
from the red volcano
reached in and covered him.
You could see the foul mood
smear across his morning face,
erasing his joy.

"What's all this noise?" he sneered. "What's a dinosaur got to do to have some peace and quiet around here?" Glancing at the red-clay paintings on the cave wall, he staggered back. "You call this *art*?" he cried. "And what's with this weather anyway? Always the same old clouds and rain. Why can't there ever be anything new? Different? Life is boring. Its a dull rut and I'm stuck in it forever."

He gave a crabby sigh.
"And look at these faces
of my children. I've never seen
such gloom. Can't a father have some happiness
when he enters a room?"
His lip curled up over his teeth
as he glowered.

We kids cowered
and hurried out the cave door to school.
I knew it would be no better there.
It was Grumble Day.
The volcano would not spare us.

The volcano smoke churned
over the school,
creating a cloud of complaining.
A raucous ruckus
of whines and gripes
rose up from the classroom
like outlaw birds on the rampage.

"I've never liked books,"
Tyrannosaurus Rex moaned,
tearing one up with his teeth.
"I hate reading.
Stories are stupid.
What's the use?
And I don't care at all for pencils."
He scowled,
snapping the pencil in two
and spitting the splinters on the stone floor.

"Homemade dolls are dumb,"
Sara Triceratops screeched.
"Stone heads and snake skin dresses.
They're nothing but messes anyway.
I'd rather have a real one
from the Dino-Mart.
Not this sorry one my mother
made especially for me."
She threw the doll in a pile
where its head cracked.

"Yuck!!! This food is the worst!" cried Monte Brontosaurus as he opened his lunch. "How can I munch on this garbage sandwich my grandfather got up early to make for me at dawn?"

Even Mr. Allosaurus
was drenched in the lousy gray
grumble-gloom.
We were all quiet when he loomed
in the door of the room.
He opened his gaping jaws
as if to growl.
We slunk down
but he stopped himself –
and just barely baring his teeth
in a reptile hiss, he said quietly,
"I've never much cared for this desk."

He slumped into his rock-chair.
"It's cramped."
Then he put his head down on a book
and sighed, breathing in more
of the bad red smoke.
"I don't like chalk either,"
he groaned.
"What's the point
of anything?"

Ashes began to drift down
from the volcano.
We dragged ourselves
out to the playground
in a flurry of fights,
a tangle of tripping,
numerous name-calling,
stuck-out tongues,
teasing tears,
and even some cheating.
Recess was rotten
under the grumble cloud
that was ruining the day.

I couldn't even bring myself to play.
I kicked a rusty swing
and slouched down under the gray ash
that was dusting the once-wondrous world.

That's when the blue lightning bolt
cracked across the sky.
Thunder followed,
rolling, tumbling.
We all looked up
as large rainsplats began to drip,
drop, dance
down on the ashy ground.

Down it splashed,
slished and slashed.
It washed the volcano's ash from our scales,
slithering over our reptile skin,
cleansing our spikes and fins.
It tickled us back
to our happy old selves.

We jumped to catch the rain
in our giant mouths.
We twirled in the twisting wind
that was washing us clean.
We pounded through puddles
as the muddle of Grumble Day
was wiped out by one good rain.

All together we shouted,
"We love bad weather!
Hooray for the rain
that has brought an end
to Grumble Day again!"

High above the gleaming palms,
the volcano hissed once,
shuddered, then stopped
spewing
its smoke.

The world looked different,
as we danced home.
Our dark trance was wiped away.
Things looked different
to our fresh eyes.
Things we thought were dumb or dull
glowed as if we'd never seen them before.

Stones glistened like gems
on the path.
Shade felt cool-delicious
on our scales.
Wildflowers we'd seen all our lives
looked like large faces
grinning at us.
Trees we'd taken for granted
arched over us with friendly arms.

Rex found a book
and sat down under a palm,
amazed at the story.
He flipped pages madly in a wild daze.

Sara wrapped her doll's head in twine
and made a new head of hair
from the frazzled string.
"It's good
to mend a thing," she said.

We could even see Mr. Allosaurus through the cave school window, wiping his desk clean.
He gazed happily around the classroom after a good day's work.

Heading home, I'd never seen the world shine
in quite this way.
"But nothing is really different,"
I said. I paused
on the path to notice
a view I'd never seen before
though I went this way
every day.

"Is it just the way
I'm noticing the plain old good
of the same old world
I felt so grumbly about before?"

And all that night I noticed the glowing
of everyday things
I'd forgotten to be grateful for:
a smile, a touch,
a comfy couch,
the swish of leaves,
the voices of my brothers
(not yelling!),
the gleam of a stone,
a warm cave,
a special star

far over the volcano (silent now),
my father's snore,
my own footprint,
cool wind,
slice of moon,
old tune,
legs that dance and leap,
and the dreams that come
when you're deep asleep.

I was even grateful
for Grumble Day
and the washing rain
that showed me the wonder and surprise
in all the plain old things
shining right before
my eyes.